THE BIG PAYOFF

Junior Discovers Integrity

by **Dave Ramsey**

Collect all of the *Junior's Adventures* books!

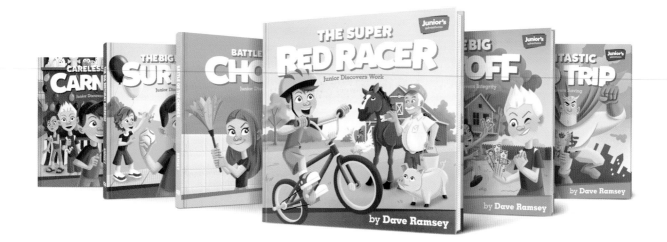

The Big Payoff: Junior Discovers Integrity
© 2015 Lampo Licensing, LLC
Published by Ramsey Press, The Lampo Group, Inc.
Brentwood, TN 37027

For more information on Dave Ramsey, visit daveramsey.com or call 888.227.3223.

Editors: Amy Parker, Jen Gingerich
Project Management: Preston Cannon, Bryan Amerine and Mallory Darcy
Illustrations: Greg Hardin, John Trent and Kenny Yamada
Art Direction: Luke LeFevre, Brad Dennison and Chris Carrico

DEDICATION

To my parents, Tom and Millie—

You taught me to work for what I want and never take what isn't mine. I remember when I was four years old and I took a candy bar from the grocery store.

You made me return it to the store manager. I was embarrassed, but I learned the lesson.

Thank you, Mom and Dad, for teaching me genuine integrity.

—Dave

"Race ya to Ida's!"
Junior yelled over his shoulder.

"Oh no you don't!" Maddie ran to catch up.

"Hey, wait up!" Billy called.

It was Friday, and that meant
after-school treats at Ida's Ice Palace.

"Thanks, Ms. Ida!" Maddie said before slurping her Galaxy Grape.

"See you next week, kids!" Ms. Ida waved with one hand while wiping the counter with the other.

As Junior got close to their bench outside, he noticed something shiny on the ground.

"It's . . . a money clip! And money!" he tried to whisper.

Billy stooped down beside the bench. "Look! Here's more!"

"It's all over the place!" Maddie squealed. She was grabbing it by the handful.

Huffing and puffing, the three bounded up the ladder of Junior's treehouse. When Maddie reached the top, she saw the boys spreading out the money on the floor. "How much do you think it is?" she whispered.

"I'm counting," Junior mouthed.

"Why are we whispering?" Billy asked.

"Whoa! Two hundred forty dollars!"
Junior was no longer whispering.

Maddie thought for a second, then blurted,
"That's eighty dollars each!"

"Yes!" Billy pumped his fist.
"The new Dollar Bill's
Adventures game
is *mine*!"

Maddie saw the sinking sun through the treehouse window. "I have *got* to get home. But let's meet first thing in the morning, 'kay?"

"Deal," Billy agreed.

"I'll hide the money until then."
Junior knelt on the floor, looking from
side to side, and opened a wooden trap
door in the floor.

Maddie smiled at the two boys. "See you tomorrow."

At dinner that evening, Junior stared out the window, ignoring his full plate.

"Junior . . ." Mom tried to get his attention. "Junior, how was your day?"

"Hmm? Oh, it was great," he answered, waking from his daydream.
"After school we went to Ida's. Then we found a bunch of money on
the ground outside!"

"Really?" Mom asked.

Dad's eyebrows went up. "What are you going to do with it?"

"I was thinking about a new skateboard." Junior couldn't keep
from smiling.

Mom and Dad exchanged concerned glances.

"Well, did you think about who might have lost the money?" Mom asked.

"I know if I had lost something," Dad added, "I would be really glad if someone returned it."

Junior now seemed to be very interested in his plate.

"I trust you, Junior," Dad said, putting a hand on his son's shoulder. "I know you'll do the right thing."

That night, Junior had a hard time falling asleep. He kept hearing those words from his dad over and over again.

I know you'll do the right thing....

Do the right thing....

The right thing....

The words echoed in Junior's dreams as he slept. He tossed and turned all night.

As he wandered through the store with his friends the next morning, all Junior could think about was who had lost that money.

"For the treehouse!" Maddie announced, holding up a cool, new radio. Billy already had the new Dollar Bill's Adventures game in hand.

"Hey, guys," Junior began, "I think we should do something different with the money."

"Oh right!" Maddie agreed. "Like if we put it all together, we could—"

"No," Junior looked at Maddie, then at Billy. "I think we should try to find out who lost it."

Maddie frowned and Billy sighed. They both knew that Junior was right.

Later that afternoon, Junior's mom handed him her phone. "It's for you, Junior. It's a Mr. Webb. He saw the sign you posted at Ida's about the money."

"Oh, uh, hello? . . . Yes sir. . . . Yes sir, the money clip too. . . . Um, let me see. Mom, would you take us over near Ida's to meet Mr. Webb?"

Mom nodded, and just a few minutes later, Junior and his friends were shaking hands with Mr. Webb by the very bench where they had first found the money.

"It's so nice to meet young people with such integrity," Mr. Webb said, putting his money clip in his pocket. "It must've been difficult to do the right thing when you could have easily spent the money yourself."

"You have no idea," Junior said. Maddie and Billy nodded their heads in agreement.

"Well, I have a little surprise for you all. Come on."

Mr. Webb led
them across
the street, past
Ms. Ida's, and
to the toy store.
"This," he said,
waving his arms,
"is my store. And
as a thank-you
for what you've done,
you can choose
anything you'd like."

Billy's mouth hung open,
frozen, as he stared at the store.

"Wha? You? I—I mean,
thank you!" Junior answered.

Maddie began jumping up and down.

"Okay, okay, you're all very welcome." Mr. Webb chuckled. "I just want you to always remember that your integrity is worth so much more than money." He stepped back and smiled at the three of them. "Now, go on. Pick out something you really like."

"What a week!" Billy said.

"Yeah, who would've believed one little choice could make such a big difference," Maddie said, trying to find some music on her new radio.

"Well, I know one thing's for sure," Junior said,
  hanging a toy store flyer to the wall with a thumbtack.
"Having integrity sure does pay off!"

That was one **truth** none of them would ever forget.